SIBLINGS

AYUSH SINGH

ISBN 979-888591727-8

I dedicate this book to all the 'SIBLINGS'. The relation which can't be describe by words. The relationship between siblings is a very important relationship. "The sibling relationship is one of the longest lasting relationships in most people's lives, and one of the most prevalent". Although this relationship is almost always a friendly one during adulthood, the childhood and adolescent relationship is usually hostile. Sibling rivalries during adolescence and childhood usually occur because of a strong amount of jealousy towards a younger sibling who appears to be receiving the full amount of attention from the parents. The three most important factors that impact the sibling relationship are birth order, age, and the parent-child or parent-parent relationships.

Birth order of siblings can play a huge role in explaining the aggression that some siblings have towards each other. Birth order is one's position in a family. For example, one is the first-born child or one is the middle child. According to Lorie M. Sutter, "Through your position in the family (birth order) you develop your behavior pattern, way of thinking, and emotional response. Your birth order helps determine your expectations, your strategies for dealing with people, and your weaknesses". Studies have shown that most first-born children are perfectionists, goal setters, and they are responsible people who obey rules. In contrast, his sibling, the second or last-born child, is usually an outgoing risk-taker who questions authority. If these characteristics are true of the two siblings, it is easy to understand why the two would not get along all of the time.

Contents

One Sunday afternoon I was sitting drinking coffee at the same time, after many years, my aun came in our house we were all very happy to see her she brought gifts for all of us after a while I left that room in another room I had to do my homework. After 1 hour I heard the sound of aunt crying and I gave water to her when she drank the water then I asked what happened why are you crying, then she said that his brother will not be able to come to Rakhi even this year, he has not come for the last 4 years.

I asked why would there be any reason, she said that her mother's death was very early when Auntie was in class 10, since then she is taking care of her brother he got his brother married But after marriage, there was a fight between Auntie and her brother's wife, due to which she separated about her wife, And Aunt Mary is still single because she hasn't married

Acknowledgements

I'm extremely grateful to all the sisters who always care for their brothers without expecting something.........

Prologue

Siblings is not an only relation between brother and sister, it's an emotion it's a feeling which can't be described by words. The relation which is better than best friends and like a relation between mother and son. The guys which get an elder sister are worlds luckiest person ever if you have a elder sister it means that you have a second mother who always care for you from your birth to your death. But in today's generation the peoples can't love their sisters. The love and emotion for their sister or from sister to their brothers is almost extinct from earth. The main reason is technology like phones and laptops, social medias. The peoples have the time to tag their sister in siblings love videos, but they don't have the time to spend with their sister.

1

About Siblings

Siblings is not an only relation between brother and sister, it's an emotion it's a feeling which can't be described by words. The relation which is better than best friends and like a relation between mother and son. The guys which get an elder sister are worlds luckiest person ever if you have a elder sister it means that you have a second mother who always care for you from your birth to your death. But in today's generation the peoples can't love their sisters. The love and emotion for their sister or from sister to their brothers is almost extinct from earth. The main reason is technology like phones and laptops, social medias. The peoples have the time to tag their sister in siblings love videos, but they don't have the time to spend with their sister.

2

A story from My Dad on 'SIBLINGS'

When I was a kid my father told me a story of their generation, that their generation was much better than ours generation, but I won't believe that I always told him that no our generation is best because in your generation there is nothing advanced but In our generation we have best smartphones which have latest features we have much more things to entertain us, after that I asked a question from my dad that at your time how would you spend your time? Then my father tells me that in our generation we are spent our times with our family specially with our cousins and siblings.

We went everyday playgrounds and played a lot of things even you can't know the names of the games which we played daily.

In those days we spent minimum 3-4 hours with our siblings because we don't have social medias at that time. But I am not believing that our generation is not good.... After some years I realized yes, my dad was right....

3
Infancy and childhood

A relationship begins with the introduction of two siblings to one another. Older siblings are often made aware of their soon-to-be younger brother or sister at some point during their mother's pregnancy, which may help facilitate adjustment for the older child and result in a better immediate relationship with the newborn. Early in development, interactions can contribute to the older sibling's social aptitude and cognitively stimulate the younger sibling.

Older siblings even adapt their speech to accommodate for the low language comprehension of the younger sibling, much like parents do with baby talk. Even as siblings age and develop, there is considerable stability in their relationships from infancy through middle childhood, during which positive and negative interactions remain constant in frequency.

4
Adulthood and old age

When siblings reach adulthood, it is more likely that they will no longer live in the same place and that they will become involved in jobs, hobbies that they do not share and therefore cannot use to relate to one another. Despite these factors, siblings often maintain a relationship through adulthood and even old age.Sisters are most likely to maintain contact with one another, Brothers are least likely to contact one another frequently.

Communication is especially important when siblings do not live near one another. Communication may take place in person, over the phone, by mail, and with increasing frequency, by means of online communication such as email and social networking. Marriage of one sibling may either strengthen or weaken the sibling bond.

5
Why Siblings are Important?

Sibling relationships are emotionally powerful and critically important not only in childhood but over the course of a lifetime. Siblings are important because there is not much difference in their age due to which they are quite comfortable with each other and if siblings relationship is good then they can share all their secrets If we don't have siblings, we will find it boring, with this we will have to share our secrets with someone outside and they can also blackmail us later and we can pass time by playing with our siblings and generally siblings are our crime partner and also they help us to do our homework And they can also blackmail us later and we can pass time by playing with our siblings.

Having a sister or brother promotes happiness and may even decrease negative emotions, even they will make us happier even if we are no in a good mood.And a report has shown that it is better if the sister is an elder sibling.They cement your attitude towards the opposite gender.She's the first to give you a dose of tough love. She's seen you at your worst and at your best, and she loves you anyway.

6

A story by an author

In this story the name of the younger brother is Ayush and the name of the elder sister is Simran. When I was 5 years old then one day I asked my friend how do you play cricket so well? Then he said that my brother taught me then slowly I started feeling that brother would have been better than sister and when my aunt's son used to come, I used to have a lot of fun with him. But as I grew older I realized that sister is much better than the brother.

Once upon a time my aunt's son made a false complaint to my mother about me, due to which

I was scold by my mom, On the other hand, I threw my pencil box in the drain, my elder sister told my mother that I means elder sister dropped the box.It happened 3-4 times that I fell in the drain while playing, then my sister took me out of the drain and took a bath as a mother bathes her child.Earlier I didn't like my sister at all but as I grow up I love my sister probably more than myself. My mother tells me that when my sister was 8 years old, then our first rakhi was at such a young age, sistertook clothes for me from her pocket money.

Sister used to steal father's money and then we used to eat chips and chocolates from that money had a lot of fun. My school used to be in the morning at that time, then mother could not get up many times and in early mornings all shops was close waking up in the morning my sister used to make tasty tiffin for me. Then many times my school bag was torn, so sister used to sew my bag with the money taught by her tuition or gave me a new bag, I still keep that bag, it is very precious for me because that bag sister gave with her first tuition money.

Whenever there used to be a fight between me and my sister, I used to think that I wish I could go to a relative's house or my sister would go.But when my sister got her dream job and posting was out of state, my eyes were filled with tears when we went to drop her at the airport. Then I came to know the value of Didi, earlier my project used to done by my sister, but I have to do everything because of sister out of state.I feel all alone after Didi goes out of city.

'WE DON'T VALUE WHAT WE HAVE'

7

Toxic Things Siblings Do or Say

1. "Making fun of each other. Don't get me wrong, sometimes it can be really funny, but it all depends on the time and place."

2.Competing for your parent's approval and always trying to 'one-up' each other and be better."

3."Overprotecting one sibling 'because they're the baby in the family' and being rude to the other siblings."

4. "Constantly commenting on weight and making fat jokes."

"As someone who always struggled with body dysmorphia and comparison to my very skinny sister, some brothers making jokes about their sisters weight has always triggered me, and it caused major mental damage."

5. "Forcing one sibling (especially common with daughters) to be the responsible/clean one and letting the other(s) get away with never doing chores or helping around the house."

6."Older siblings blaming the younger sibling for stealing all the attention. It's rough and unfair."

7. "Teasing your sibling even when you tell them to stop. They know what you're scared of and will use it against you."

8."Judging yourself against your sibling's success, or thinking you're in some kind of competition with them."

9."Using put-downs and insults as jokes. My sister never compliments anything I do — just makes jokes at my expense. My brother has always said he was the good-looking one, my sister the smart one, and I had the scraps."

10."Choosing to not respect boundaries — and more so, parents not encouraging siblings to respect each other's boundaries. It's one thing to cross a boundary on accident, but it's another to do it on purpose and with the intent of truly upsetting someone you care about."

11.Making it the oldest sibling's job to maintain the sibling relationship."

12."Making most things fall on the oldest siblings in general, especially as adults."

13."When you tell your sibling something in confidence, and they tell the rest of the family, or their friends."

8
What would a gap of two or three years be like?

What would a gap of two or three years be like?

If you want to have time to enjoy each child's baby years, a two or three-year gap may suit you.

By the time your second baby arrives you should have caught up on sleep. Your first child will have become increasingly independent too.

Your first or oldest child may be out of nappies and be happily feeding and dressing herself. She may also be making her needs clear with an extensive vocabulary. You may therefore have the energy to return to the world of sleepless nights, breastfeeding and umpteen nappies and outfits a day.

Your older child is perhaps confident and secure enough in herself to welcome a new addition. And you can imagine how she'll love being a big sister and playing with her sibling.

While your older child is at playgroup or preschool, you'll be able to enjoy individual time with your new baby.

Even so, having this age gap is still going to mean a few years before your children want to play together. The games of a five-year-old are very different from the games of a two-year-old. But a seven-year-old and a 10-year-old could have lots of fun together.

As the world of your older child expands, your newborn has to fit in with her hectic social life.

There will be interrupted feeds and sleeps, as your baby will probably need to come along when you take your toddler to playgroup or other activities.

Taking a baby along to toddler classes isn't always easy and like many mums you may need to make alternate childcare arrangements for your baby if things get too hectic.

9

What would a gap of five years or more be like?

—♡—

Like some parents, you may feel that if you want to cherish the baby and preschooler years of your individual children, a gap of five or more years could be perfect. The baby years of your oldest will be long gone and she'll be settled into her school.

It's likely that you'll be more relaxed this time and less likely to worry about the little things. Your older children have left nappies, sleepless nights, teething and tantrums far behind. You'll probably have more time and energy to enjoy a baby. You'll be able to give your new baby lots of individual time if your eldest is busy at school and with their social life.

Your older child may enjoy being involved with a baby, though be careful not to treat your eldest as a mini-parent. When they do play together, your heart will probably burst while you watch them. And returning to mum and toddler activities can be wonderful and help you re-live all the fun.

Even so, having one child followed by a long gap before another child can be like having two singletons. They may grow up having little in common and the eldest may even have left home for college by the time your youngest is still at school.

Your older child may find it difficult to suddenly have to share your attention. And there will be days when your toddler has a tantrum when you are trying to help your older child with homework. Or days when you feel torn in two when your baby is fussy due to teething and your eldest wants to call her group of friends over for a party.

There is no perfect gap that suits absolutely everyone and every age gap has its pros and cons. So it's up to you and your family to decide when the time is right for you. And remember, however much you think ahead, babies don't always turn up as planned!

10
Things To Do With your Siblings

—❦—

1. Get to know each other

You may be thinking, "Hey, I grew up with this person. I already know her better than anyone." And, in some ways, that's true — you and your sister have a history and a bond that you don't share with other people.

2. Travel together!

Whether it's a simple road trip or an international dream vacation, traveling with sisters is crazy fun. And if you no longer live with your sisters, it's a rare opportunity to spend a lot of time together.

3.Hang out with your parents.

I've stressed the importance of getting to know your siblings without your parents around, but that doesn't mean you always have to cut the 'rents out of your plans. I really love hanging out with my parents and sisters, and I'm sure my parents are relieved and amazed to see their formerly perpetually-squabbling daughters having fun together.

4.Get your DIY on.

Sisters are in that small group of loved ones that you can call on to help you paint your new living room, install floating shelves in the kitchen, or make four dozen cupcakes for your kid's Halloween party. They know they'll have fun working on crafty stuff with you (and that you'll pay back the favor someday).

5. Work Out.

Motivating oneself to exercise is always a little easier when you have a friend there to make it fun. Who better than a sister?

11

How To Get Along With Your Sister

1. Support your sister's achievements. If you want a good relationship with your sister, make her feel supported. Instead of becoming jealous over your sister's achievements, be her personal cheerleader. This will make your sister feel valued and strengthen your bond.

2.Set boundaries respectfully. Boundaries are important for any healthy relationship. Without solid boundaries, positive relationships are difficult. You are entitled to your own physical and emotional space. When your sister invades your space, let her know politely instead of responding with anger.

3.Do chores together. A great way to improve your relationship is by working together. Try to help your sister with some of her chores, and ask her for help in return. If the two of you work together on, say, the dishes, this will encourage teamwork and a sense of togetherness.

4. Treat your sister more like a friend. Many people have a tendency to take siblings for granted. You may fail to see your sister as an individual if you're used to viewing her as just another family member. Try to treat your sister as a friend. Many siblings eventually become good friends.

5.Do not be jealous of your sister's talents. Jealousy is very common in sibling relationships and can be a major cause of tension. If your sister is, for example, a bookworm, she may get a lot of attention from relatives. Instead of being jealous of this, admire your sister's talents.

6. Appereciate your sister's good quality. If you're sometimes angry with your sister, keeping her good qualities in mind can hlp. Instead of focusing on things she does that irritate you, thing about the reasons you value her.